Discovering the
TROPICAL SAVANNA

Janey Levy

PowerKiDS
press.

New York

Published in 2008 by The Rosen Publishing Group, Inc.
29 East 21st Street, New York, NY 10010

Copyright © 2008 by The Rosen Publishing Group, Inc.

First Edition

Editor: Joanne Randolph and Geeta Sobha
Book Design: Julio Gil
Photo Researcher: Nicole Pristash

Photo Credits: Cover, p.1 © Getty Images/Skip Brown; pp. 5, 6, 8, 10, 13, 14, 15, 18, 21, 25, 27, 29 © www.shutterstock.com; pp. 17, 22, 23 © Artville.

Library of Congress Cataloging-in-Publication Data

Levy, Janey.
  Discovering the tropical savanna / Janey Levy. — 1st ed.
    p. cm. — (World habitats)
  Includes index.
  ISBN-13: 978-1-4042-3783-4 (library binding)
  ISBN-10: 1-4042-3783-6 (library binding)
  1. Savanna ecology—Tropics—Juvenile literature. 2. Savannas—Tropics—Juvenile literature. I. Title.
  QH541.5.P7L48 2008
  577.4'8—dc22

                                        2006103368

Manufactured in the United States of America

Contents

What Is a Tropical Savanna?

A savanna is a type of grassland. As its name suggests, a grassland is a region where grasses are the main plants. A savanna differs from other grasslands because it also has widely scattered trees and shrubs.

There is more than one kind of savanna. This book is about tropical savannas. Tropical savannas have two seasons, a wet summer and a dry winter. They also have frequent fires that kill shrubs and young trees. Fires clear the land, leaving plenty of open land for grasses to grow. Without the

Why Are They Called "Savannas"?

The word "savanna" probably came from a Native American word that meant "land with no trees but with much grass." Over time the word came to mean "land with both grass and trees."

Most savannas have a dry season with very little rain that limits the growth of trees.

Antelope are grass-eating animals that live on the African savanna.

fires, trees and shrubs would fill the region, and it would become a forest.

Tropical savannas have existed for 20 to 25 million years. That makes them a very old biome. A biome is a community of plants and animals that live together in a region and depend on each other. Climate affects what kind of biome a region has. Let's learn more about the climate of tropical savannas.

The Climate of Tropical Savannas

The wet summer season of tropical savannas lasts six to eight months. During these months, there is plenty of rainfall. Annual rainfall varies from one tropical savanna to another. Some get as little as 10 inches (25 cm) of rain each year. Others get as much as 50 inches (127 cm) of rain.

Winter lasts four to six months. During part of this time, no rain may fall at all. Fires occur frequently during the dry season. Lightning causes some fires. People cause others.

Tropical savannas are warm throughout the year. During the warm, wet summer, the average monthly temperature ranges from 68° F (20° C) to 86° F (30° C). Even during the cooler, dry winter, temperatures still range from 50° F (10° C) to 68° F (20° C).

Where in the World Are Tropical Savannas?

Tropical savannas cover almost one-third of Earth's land surface. They are called tropical because they occur in a region of Earth called the tropics. The tropics are a very warm area around the equator. The northern edge of the tropics is a line called the Tropic of Cancer, which is about 1,622 miles (2,610 km) north of the equator. The southern edge is a line called the Tropic of Capricorn, which is about the same distance south of the equator.

Four continents have tropical savannas. They are Africa, South America, Australia, and Asia. Tropical savannas cover almost half of Africa. They extend over about 5 million square miles (13 million sq km). That area is larger than the United States! Tropical savannas cover about

Fires help keep the savannas clear of trees by destroying young trees. These fires do not harm older trees on the savanna.

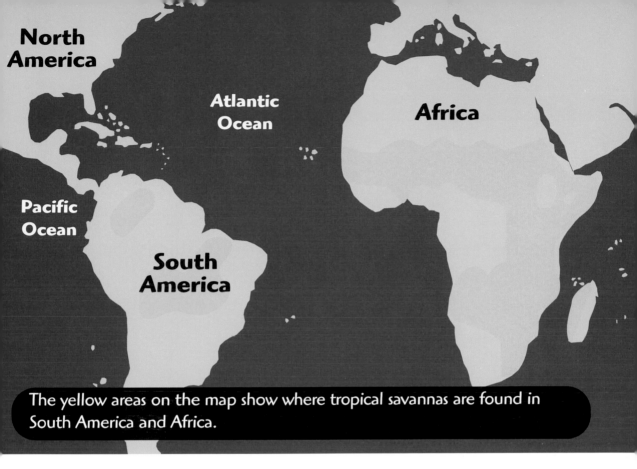

The yellow areas on the map show where tropical savannas are found in South America and Africa.

800,000 square miles (2 million sq km) of South America. They cover about one-fourth of Australia, or about 742,500 square miles (1.9 million sq km). Only a small part of the large Asian continent has tropical savannas. They cover a large area in India and a small area in Southeast Asia.

Candelabra trees can be found on savannas in Africa and South Asia. Their sap is poisonous and can produce swelling on the skin.

Tropical Savanna Plants

Grasses and forbs, which are small plants with broad leaves, are the main plants on tropical savannas. Tropical savanna grasses are quite different from the grass you see in yards or parks. These grasses are often coarse and range from 3 to 9 feet (1–3 m) or more in height. They usually grow in clumps separated by areas of bare dirt.

Africa's Toothbrush Tree

A low African savanna bush with long, arching shoots is known as the toothbrush tree. People cut off a green shoot, chew the end, and then brush their teeth with it!

There are many different tropical savanna grasses, although all types do not grow on all savannas. Some common types are Rhodes grass,

The baobab tree has tough bark that protects it from savanna fires.

The jarrah tree grows in Australia's savannas. Shown here are its spring flowers.

red oats grass, star grass, and lemongrass. Others include elephant grass, spear grass, and kangaroo grass.

   Single trees or small groups of trees dot tropical savannas. Just like the grasses, different tree species grow on different savannas. Some common trees are acacias, baobabs, eucalyptus, and palms. Others include cypress trees and nance trees, which produce tasty yellow fruit.

Tropical savanna plants have adapted to survive the long dry season and the fires. They store water and food in their roots. Some trees have thick bark to protect them from fires. Other trees lose their leaves during the dry season to keep from losing water. Some trees store water under their bark. Others have long roots that reach water deep in the ground.

The yellow kangaroo paw grows in western Australia. Its flowers are about 4 inches (10 cm) long.

Tropical Savanna Animals

There are many tropical savanna animal species, although all species do not live on all savannas. Not surprisingly many of them are grazing animals. These include zebras, buffalo, wildebeests, rhinoceroses, antelopes, and kangaroos. Other plant-eating animals include elephants, giraffes, and tapirs. Savannas also have many animals that eat the grazers and the other plant-eating animals. These include lions, leopards, hyenas, crocodiles, and jaguars.

Tropical savannas are home to many other animal species as well. These include mice, ground squirrels, warthogs, opossums, lizards, snakes, and armadillos. Many kinds of birds live in savannas, including two huge birds that cannot fly, the ostrich and the emu. Termites, beetles, grasshoppers, caterpillars, and many other insects also make their homes in savannas.

Giraffes live on the savannas of Africa. They are the world's tallest mammals.

Savanna animals have adapted to survive the dry season and fires just as savanna plants have. Large animals and birds usually migrate to other regions during the dry season. Elephants migrate, but they are also able to get water by knocking down trees that store water. Large animals and birds run or fly to escape fires. However, some birds fly toward fires. They go to eat the insects and small animals escaping the fire or that were killed by it.

A Father's Care

The male emu, not the female, sits on the eggs for two months until they hatch. During this time he may lose 20 pounds (9 kg). After the babies hatch, he takes care of them.

Small animals often stay in deep holes during the dry season and remain inactive until the rains return. They also hide in holes to escape fires.

Cheetahs are the fastest land animals. They can run as fast as 65 miles per hour (105 kmh).

The Serengeti Plain forms the southern part of the Serengeti, a large savanna in eastern Africa. Rhodes grass is the main grass. The plains have few trees because of a special feature of the soil. Less than 3 feet (1 m) below the surface is a layer almost as hard as concrete. It is called hardpan and keeps water close to the surface, which is good for grasses. However, hardpan prevents trees from growing because they cannot send roots deep down into the ground. In spite of this, some acacia trees can still grow on the Serengeti.

Three kinds of grassland are found in the Serengeti Plain. The south has short-grass plains. North and west of them are medium-grass plains. North of these are long-grass plains.

About 2 million large grazing animals live on the plains. There are 45 mammal species and about

The Serengeti Plain is found in the country of Tanzania, which is on the eastern coast of Africa.

Another name for the wildebeest is gnu. Wildebeests feed on the grasses of the Serengeti.

500 bird species. Common plains animals include lions, antelopes, wildebeests, buffalo, zebras, rhinoceroses, ostriches, lizards, snakes, and grasshoppers. You might also see elephants.

The Serengeti's famous migration of wildebeests and zebras draws thousands of visitors to the plains every year. When the dry season begins, 1 million wildebeests and 200,000 zebras migrate from the plains to the wetter northern part of the Serengeti. When the rains begin again, these huge herds return to the plains.

Forests + Elephants = Savannas

Elephants can turn forests into savannas. They do this by eating lots of tree leaves, breaking branches off trees, smashing tree trunks, stripping bark off trees, and crushing young trees.

Elephants are the largest land mammals on Earth.

Australia's Tropical Savanna

A very hot tropical savanna stretches across northern Australia. During the wet season, the temperature is usually around 86° F (30° C). However, it can get as high as 122° F (50° C)!

Plants on the Australian savanna differ from plants elsewhere. The most common tree is the eucalyptus.

Giants Roamed Here

Today Australia's savanna does not have huge mammals, but it once did. More than 40,000 years ago, kangaroos up to 10 feet (3 m) tall and wombats the size of small cars grazed here!

The hundreds of mammals, birds, reptiles, and amphibians also differ from animals elsewhere. Mammals include wombats, kangaroos, and other marsupials. Birds include emus. Among reptile species are giant crocodiles up to 26 feet (8 m) long!

Termites can build mounds as high as 19 feet (6 m).

How Do People Affect Tropical Savannas?

People have both helped and hurt tropical savannas. In some places people have played a part in creating and maintaining savannas by regularly setting fires. Fires are important to the health and survival of the savanna biome. Australia's native people, the Aborigines, have burned savannas for about 50,000 years. Fires set by people have also been important for preserving India's savannas.

People have hurt savannas in many ways. They may graze cattle and goats on the savanna. When the herds eat all the grass, the savanna becomes desert. People destroy savannas through building and farming. Some people illegally hunt savanna animals. Farmers may kill animals they believe harm their crops. New animals and plants brought into savannas may drive out the native ones. In some places tropical savannas are in danger of disappearing.

In many savanna areas, people have built farms or allowed their animals to graze, causing harm to the savannas.

Protecting Tropical Savannas

Does it matter if tropical savannas disappear? Yes, it does. Tropical savannas are home to thousands of plant and animal species. These species could vanish forever if savannas disappear.

In Africa and Australia, people who have lived on savannas for thousands of years have built up special ways of life. Those ways of life would disappear with the savannas.

What are people doing to protect tropical savannas? They are teaching others about the savannas' importance. They are establishing parks and other special areas to keep savannas safe. They work with people living around savannas to find ways to meet the people's needs and protect the savannas at the same time. With luck and hard work, this beautiful and important biome hopefully will survive.

The Masai are native people of Kenya and Tanzania.

Tropical Savanna Facts and Figures

- About two million years ago, the first humans occupied the African savanna.

- South America's largest savanna has more than 10,000 plant species.

- Lizards that are 5 feet (1.5 m) long live on Australia's savanna.

- More than 40 species of hoofed mammals can be found on Africa's savannas.

- Africa's black mamba, which is a member of the tropical savanna biome, is the world's deadliest snake.

- The Serengeti's climate, plants, and animals have hardly changed in the last one million years.

- Grasshoppers on the Serengeti eat more grass than all the large grazing animals combined.

- Dung beetles roll away up to 75 percent of all the dung on the Serengeti.

- The African elephant is the largest land animal. It weighs 6,600 to 11,800 pounds (3,000-5,400 kg).

- The zebra's stripes prevent hunting lions from seeing it at night.

Glossary

antelopes (AN-teh-lohps) Thin, fast animals found in Asia and Africa.

armadillos (ar-muh-DIH-lohz) South American mammals with small bony plates on their body and head.

dung (DUNG) Animal waste.

equator (ih-KWAY-tur) The imaginary line around Earth that separates it into two parts, northern and southern.

grazing (GRAYZ-ing) Feeding on grass.

mammal (MA-mul) A warm-blooded animal that has a backbone and hair, breathes air, and feeds milk to its young.

migrate (MY-grayt) To move from one place to another.

species (SPEE-sheez) A single kind of living thing. All people are one species.

tapirs (TAY-purz) Piglike mammals of South America and Southeast Asia.

termites (TUR-myts) Insects that live in large colonies and eat wood.

tropical (TRAH-puh-kul) Having to do with the warm parts of Earth that are near the equator.

warthogs (WORT-hogz) Wild African hogs that have large heads and long, curved teeth that stick out of their mouth.

wombats (WAHM-bats) Australian marsupials that look like bears.

Index

A
Africa, 9, 20, 28
antelopes, 16, 22
armadillos, 16
Asia, 9, 11
Australia, 9, 11, 24, 26, 28

B
biome, 6, 26, 28
birds, 16, 19, 24

E
Earth, 9
equator, 9

F
forest, 6

G
grass(es), 4, 12, 14, 20, 26
grassland(s), 4
grazing animals, 16, 20

M
mammals, 24

S
season(s), 4, 7, 15, 19, 22, 24
shrubs, 4, 6
South America, 9, 11

T
tapirs, 16
temperature(s), 7, 24
termites, 16
tree(s), 4, 6, 14–15, 19–20, 24
Tropic of Cancer, 9
Tropic of Capricorn, 9
tropics, 9

W
warthogs, 16

Web Sites

Due to the changing nature of Internet links, PowerKids Press has developed an online list of Web sites related to the subject of this book. This site is updated regularly. Please use this link to access the list:

www.powerkidslinks.com/whab/savanna